THIS BOOK BELONGS TO

_____

Thanks for letting me wear a
bin bag to my birthday party,
this one's for you, Dad, forever X
L.D.

To naughtiness, chaos and a sense of humour,
may we never lose you three.
S.P.

First published in the UK in 2022
First published in the US in 2022
by Faber and Faber Limited
Bloomsbury House,
74–77 Great Russell Street,
London WC1B 3DA
faberchildrens.co.uk

Text © Laura Dockrill, 2022
Illustrations © Sandhya Prabhat, 2022
Designed by Faber and Faber
HB ISBN 978-0-571-33508-4
PB ISBN 978-0-571-33509-1

Printed in India
2 4 6 8 10 9 7 5 3 1
The moral rights of Laura Dockrill and Sandhya Prabhat have been asserted
A CIP record for this book is available from the British Library

FSC
www.fsc.org
MIX
Paper from
responsible sources
FSC® C016779

Faber has published children's books since 1929. T. S. Eliot's *Old Possum's
Book of Practical Cats* and Ted Hughes' *The Iron Man* were amongst the first.
Our catalogue at the time said that 'it is by reading such books that children
learn the difference between the shoddy and the genuine'. We still believe in
the power of reading to transform children's lives. All our books are chosen
with the express intention of growing a love of reading, a thirst for knowledge
and to cultivate empathy. We pride ourselves on responsible editing. Last but
not least, we believe in kind and inclusive books in which all children feel
represented and important.

PUNK ROCKER POODLE

LAURA DOCKRILL · SANDHYA PRABHAT

faber

NO 'PLEASE'
NO SMILE
NO *HELLO*

NO SOCKS!
NO FROCKS!
DON'T THINK SO

AND NONE OF YOU
LOT AT SOFT PLAY,

NO!

GOOD BO

~~SCRIBBLE~~ ~~SCRIBBLING~~
Perfect poochie
Smoochie woochie
Cutesie wutsie

NO BED!

ABSOLUTELY NOT!

NO SLEEP!
WON'T SLEEP!

NO.

NO.

NO!

Oi? Oi? Oi? Oi? You? You? You?

Maybe, just a small tincy cuddle . . .

A **SCRATCH**
on the belly?

Those lovely new
JIM-JAMS

A **CARTOON**
on the telly?

And what about my dummy too
and where is my teddy?

and a little hot milk there
wouldn't go amiss

and I suppose I wouldn't mind
just a little goodnight kiss

oooooo
how cosy
how wonderful is this?

SNORE...
SNORE...
SNORE...

see what
tomorrow
brings.